The Pie-Eating Contest

Written by Mick Gowar

Illustrated by François Hall

WAYLAND

It was supper time in Cactus Thorn,
but Deputy Pete didn't feel like eating.

5

"It's your favourite – bacon and beans," said Sheriff Stan.

"I'm not hungry," said Pete.

"But it's the pie-eating contest on Saturday," said Sheriff Stan. "You're the champion. You need to keep up your strength!"

Deputy Pete sighed. "I'll go for a walk. Walking always makes me hungry."

"It's Deputy Pete," whispered
Dudley Dalton.
"Quick, put this sack over his
head," said Ma Dalton.

They grabbed Pete and tied him up.
Then they took him to their shack
in the woods.

"Let me go!" shouted Pete.
"Help me!"

"I'll let you go on Saturday," said Ma Dalton. "Promise. As soon as my son Dudley has won the pie-eating contest."

"Can I have something to eat?"
asked Pete.

"Yes," said Ma. "You can have bread and water."

"Is that all?" asked Pete.

"Yes," said Ma, and Dudley and Ma tucked into their pies.

Next morning, it was the same.
"Can I have some breakfast,
please?" asked Pete. "I'm hungry."

"You can have bread and water,"
said Ma Dalton.

All day long Pete's tummy rumbled and grumbled. He was starving!

"Do you want some supper?" asked Ma Dalton.

"Yes!" said Pete. "I'm SO hungry. What are we having?"

"Bread and water," said Ma Dalton.

19

Next morning Pete was
EVEN MORE hungry.

"Bye, Pete," said Ma Dalton.
"Dudley and I are off to
the contest!"

Pete had eaten nothing but bread and water for three days. He was so thin that his hands slipped out of the ropes Ma Dalton had tied him up with.

Pete ran all the way back to Cactus Thorn and was just in time for the pie-eating contest!

"Welcome back!" said Sheriff
Stan. "Did your long walk
make you hungry?"

"I'm so hungry I could eat a cow!"
said Pete. "A cow pie!"

"Ready... Steady... EAT!"
The contest began.

Pete ate one pie. Then another. And another. He kept going and going until he had eaten all the pies on the table!

Dudley Dalton couldn't keep up with him. Ma Dalton was very cross indeed!

Sheriff Stan climbed up onto the stage. "And the winner of the pie-eating contest is..." he shouted. There was a drum roll. "...Deputy Pete!"

The crowd went wild.

"I owe it all to you, Ma Dalton," said Pete. "Three days on bread and water can make a cowboy very, VERY hungry!"

START READING is a series of highly enjoyable books for beginner readers. **The books have been carefully graded to match the Book Bands widely used in schools.** This enables readers to be sure they choose books that match their own reading ability.

Look out for the Band colour on the book in our Start Reading logo.

The Bands are:

Pink Band 1

Red Band 2

Yellow Band 3

Blue Band 4

Green Band 5

Orange Band 6

Turquoise Band 7

Purple Band 8

Gold Band 9

START READING books can be read independently or shared with an adult. They promote the enjoyment of reading through satisfying stories supported by fun illustrations.

Mick Gowar has written more than 70 books for children, and likes to visit schools and libraries to give readings and lead workshops. He has also written plays and songs, and has worked with many orchestras. Mick writes his books in a shed in Cambridge.

François Hall loves the Wild West, but lives in a terraced 'ranch' down in the South. As well as being quick on the draw, he also designs knitting books. Cowboys often knitted on the homestead and poor Dudley has to wear very itchy underpants made by Ma Dalton!